D1300676

# YAO BAI AND THE EGG PIRATES

Written by Tim J. Myers
Illustrated by Bonnie Pang

WEST
MARGIN
PRESS®

Text © 2019 by Tim J. Myers

Illustrations © 2019 by Bonnie Pang

Editor: Michelle McCann

Library of Congress Cataloguing-in-Publication Data is
on file.

ISBN 9781513261447 (hardcover)
ISBN 9781513261454 (ebook)

Printed in China
22 21 20 19 1 2 3 4 5

Published by
West Margin Press®

WEST
MARGIN
PRESS®
WestMarginPress.com

Proudly distributed by
Ingram Publisher Services.

WEST MARGIN PRESS
Publishing Director: Jennifer Newens
Marketing Manager: Angela Zbornik
Editor: Olivia Ngai
Design & Production: Rachel Lopez Metzger

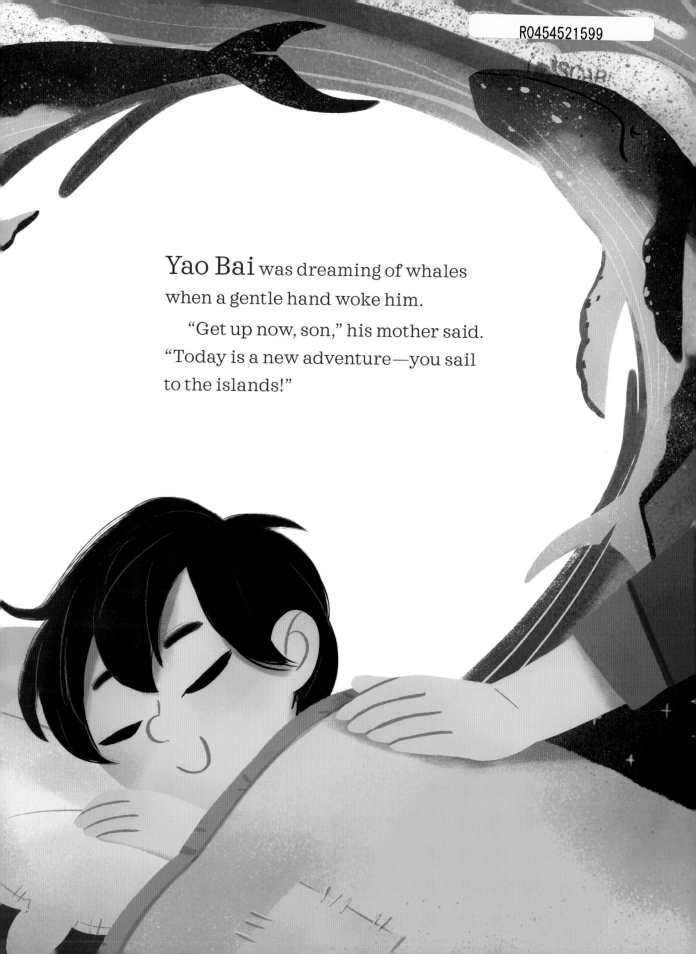

**Yao Bai** was dreaming of whales when a gentle hand woke him.

"Get up now, son," his mother said. "Today is a new adventure—you sail to the islands!"

Rubbing his hands for warmth in the dawn chill, Yao hurried to the beach. There his father and uncle were preparing their small boat. Out across the shallow bay, sunlight flooded the world.

After years of famine and war, Yao's famil~~~ed the~~~~~~ ocean~~
from China to "Gold Mountain," their name f~~~~~ Yao ha~~~
been sad to leave China, but sadder still that th~~~ whales
during their long journey. Now they lived in a fi~~~mp nestled
in upper San Francisco Bay, north of the city.

The boy from next door came running. "Going shrimping, Yao?"

"No, Kwon," Yao said. "We're sailing out on the ocean to the islands where seabirds lay eggs, to collect them for all those hungry gold miners. We'll make a fortune!"

"Yao—we need you," his father said sharply. Yao ran to help.

"What about pirates?" Kwon asked. "They might steal your eggs!"

"Our fishing tax is due," Yao's father said, "and we must send more money to our family in Guangdong. Miners pay a lot for eggs. As for pirates—we'll just have to take our chances."

Yao's mother came running. "Don't forget to rub Pu-Tai's belly for luck!" she called. Yao's uncle laughed, but they each held the small statue of the god.

As Yao rubbed, he prayed silently: *Give us good fortune—and please keep pirates away!*

"When you return," his mother said, "I'll mix the eggs with shrimp."
She winked at Yao.

"Shrimp foo young—my favorite!" he cried.

Soon they dragged the boat into the low surf and set their sail. Before long they rounded the Marin headland and made for the open ocean. Yao gazed across the water at San Francisco, with its house-covered hills and the forest of ship masts crowding its piers.

Current, wind, and tide moved them quickly out of the bay. The morning land breeze was behind them, the seas gentle. To the west they could see the islands—the Farallons—twenty-six miles away, their stony points clear against the blue horizon.

"Yao," his father said, "we have to watch for pirates. Stay alert."

"Yes, Father." Yao shivered.

When they reached the main island, the sun was high overhead. "We only want murre eggs," Yao's uncle said. "The shells are thick, hard to break. The birds fly off when humans come, leaving the eggs unprotected. And the eggs are so big, one can feed three people!"

"Yao," his father said, "you gather near the boat where it's safer. We'll go higher." Soon Yao was scrambling over the rocks, filling his basket, admiring the graceful shapes of the speckled eggs.

In a few hours their boat was full and they set sail for home, the eggs clicking gently against each other with the rocking of the hull.

For a time they watched the land grow larger as the west wind drove them on. Yao was getting sleepy . . . when something caught his eye.

"Sails!" he yelled, pointing east. His father jumped up.

"Pirates?" Yao asked fearfully. His uncle nodded.

"All that work for nothing," Yao's uncle added, shaking his head.

Yao looked at their precious cargo. Suddenly an idea came to him. "We can hide the eggs!"

"Where?" his uncle said. "We couldn't hide anything on such a small boat!"

In a rush, Yao explained his plan.

"I never would have thought of that!" said his uncle with a laugh. Even Yao's father smiled. They quickly got to work.

The pirate boat was still a half mile off when they finished. Not an egg could be seen.

"Now," Yao's father said, "we pretend to fish."

When the larger boat drew up, Yao could see hard-looking faces.

"Chinaman!" a sailor called out. "What're you doin' here?"

Yao saw his father wince angrily at the hated word, and noticed how his uncle's jaw tightened.

"Fishing," Yao's father answered in English.

"Just fishin'?" the man asked suspiciously.

"Not much else to do out here," said Yao's uncle.

The man glared. "You givin' me lip, boy?"

"No," said Yao's uncle, looking straight into the man's eyes.

"Ease up, Jeffries." An older man emerged from behind a pile of baskets. He looked their boat over carefully.

"Why don't you cross on over, make sure
they're tellin' the truth," he said quietly.

Jeffries gave a nasty smile.

But just as he lifted his leg to step
onto the boat, a great watery
whoosh filled the air.

When Yao looked, he thought
his heart would stop.

An immense humpback whale, its dark skin
specked with white barnacles, lifted itself high out
of the waves. Then it slumped sideways, falling back
with a huge splash that left both boats rocking madly.

The men grabbed for something to hang on to as the boats pitched dangerously close to each other. Finally the rocking eased.

"We don't need no damage to our boat," the pirate boss said. "They ain't got eggs. Let's clear out." He stared hard at Yao's father. "And we don't need your kind around here, understand?"

His heart thumping, Yao watched the big boat pull away.

Once the pirate sails disappeared, Yao helped haul in their nets. As the eggs rose dripping from the water, Yao laughed with joy.

The eggs felt cold to the touch as they lowered them gingerly back into the hull. Only three were broken. Gulls screeched and dove as Yao's uncle threw the shells overboard.

"Good thing we rubbed Pu-Tai's belly," said Yao's uncle. "It brought us luck after all!"

"Yao did too," said Yao's father, smiling. "I'm proud of you, my son."

Soon they tied up at a wharf in the city and Yao's father sold the eggs, stuffing more money than Yao had ever seen into his worn purse. Keeping a few eggs for themselves, they sailed home.

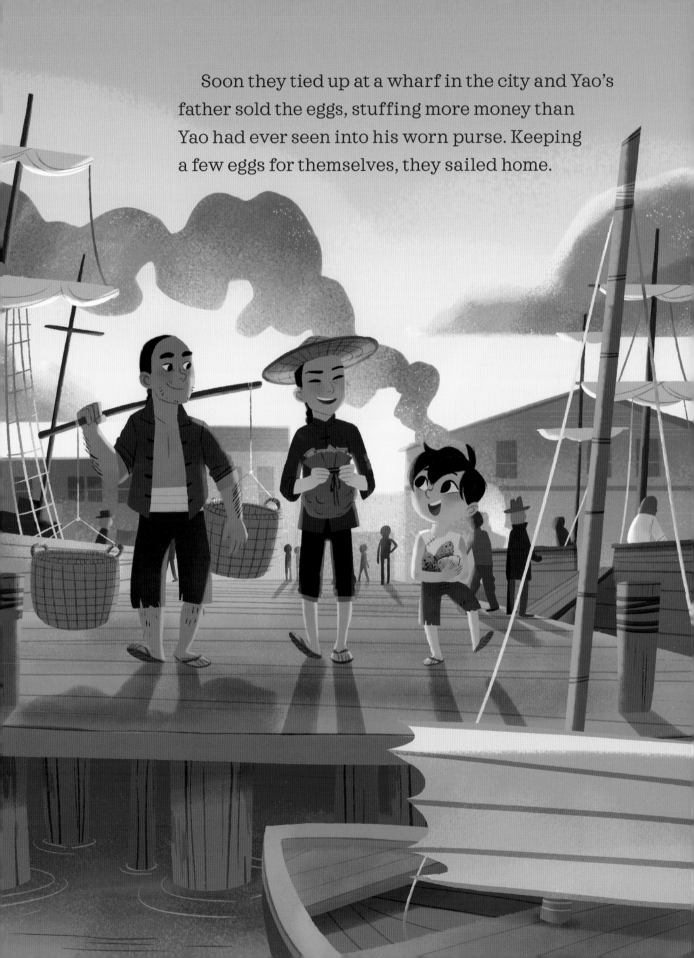

As they neared the beach, all the families came running.
The twilight was soon full of the mouthwatering smell
of shrimp foo young.

Sitting around a fire, everyone ate till they could eat no more,
and listened to the story of Yao's delicious trickery ten times over.
Then they talked and laughed till the moon was high.

It was late when Yao finally dropped into bed, happy and exhausted. "When you woke this morning," his mother said, tucking him in, "did you ever think this day would be so wonderful?"

"It *was* wonderful!" Yao murmured. "I . . . saw . . . a whale!"

Then he slept, a bit of shrimp foo young still clinging to his lip.

## AUTHOR'S NOTE

This story began over a decade ago when I took a cruise to the Farallon Islands. Most of the year these great rocks are pounded by surf, blasted by winds, or lost in fog. But we circled the "Devil's Teeth" on a sunny day, surrounded by humpbacks, blue whales, and thousands of seabirds.

Native Americans avoided the Farallons, considering them the Land of the Dead where spirits gathered after death. European explorers came for seals and eggs. But when the Gold Rush began in 1848, egg gathering became big business. Miners flooded California, and supplying them with food was a challenge. The presence of so many eggs just offshore brought eggers. Common murre eggs were the best—they had shells thick enough to survive the rough trip to the mainland and were much larger than chicken eggs.

In 1851 David "Doc" Robinson formed the Pacific Egg Company and claimed all the eggs. Others heard about his profits, and the "egg rush" was on. In 1863 armed competitors rowed out in three boats. When the Pacific eggers confronted them, the men opened fire. By the end of the "Egg War," one man from each side was dead. And as Yao Bai discovers in the story, there really were egg pirates who stole what others gathered.

Eggers could remove as many as 50,000 eggs in a single season. The murre population dropped from 4 million to 6,000. Fortunately, chicken production in nearby Petaluma increased, making Farallon eggs less profitable. The islands became a national wildlife refuge in 1969, and murre numbers have rebounded, as have the numbers of elephant seals and fur seals, which had disappeared from the islands.

But my story isn't only about eggs. At the start of the Gold Rush, China was embroiled in the Taiping Rebellion. During this uprising—the worst civil war in history—more than 20 million

died. Not surprisingly, many Chinese sought their fortunes in California. Chinese fishing villages sprung up around the Bay Area and beyond. My story was also inspired by a visit to China Camp, a beautiful state park in Marin County, once home to shrimping families like Yao's.

Immigration is the story of America, and Chinese immigrants are central to that story. Chinese families, however, faced many injustices. Racism and resentment of their successes led to restrictions on fishing and exporting shrimp. But in 1882 the Chinese Exclusion Act, the first significant law to restrict immigration to the U.S., banned all Chinese from entering. Chinese people who lived here were even attacked. This was an ugly chapter in our history.

My characters are fictional, but the history around them is real. I think it's possible that Chinese fishermen might have gathered eggs from the Farallons. After all, Chinese miners often found success on sites Americans had abandoned as worthless. I wrote this story to highlight the courage and intelligence these early immigrants showed in the face of so many obstacles. I want to honor all those whose lives have gone into making the shining fabric that is America.

For more information, young readers can check out these links:
- Search PBS.org for "PBS American Experience Gold Rush," which has an excellent section on the Gold Rush and Chinese involvement in it.
- Search SocialStudiesForKids.com for "Gold Rush."
- Teachers can search PBS.org for "Teacher's Guide: Suggestions for Active Learning."

For the full bibliography, please check out my website, TimMyersStorySong.com.

## ACKNOWLEDGMENTS

I want to thank the many individuals who helped me with this book. My editor Michelle McCann was fantastic, as was the whole team at West Margin Press—thank you Jennifer Newens, Olivia Ngai, Rachel Metzger, and Kathy Howard. (The story appeared in a different form in the May 2012 *Cricket Magazine*, and I'm also grateful to Lonnie Plecha, my editor then.) My colleagues Dr. Weijia Shang and Dr. Thomas Plante of Santa Clara University helped in crucial ways, as did others who commented on the manuscript, like Chu-Chih, Li-Li Sheng, and Nancy Wang of the fabulous storytelling duo Eth-Noh-Tec. I'm especially indebted to historian Connie Young Yu of History/San Jose, author of *Chinatown, San José, U.S.A.*, Historian of the Chinese Historical and Cultural Project, and Board Member Emeritus of the Chinese Historical Society of America, for both her reading of the manuscript and additional historical information. And I can hardly say enough about Bonnie Pang's superb illustrations.

As always, I'm also endlessly grateful to my family.

**TIM J. MYERS** is a writer, songwriter, and storyteller. He's the author of seventeen children's books and four books of poetry for adults. His *Basho and the Fox* made the *New York Times* best-seller list for children's books and was chosen by *Smithsonian Magazine* as a notable book. Myers lives in Santa Clara, CA, where he's a senior lecturer at Santa Clara University. Visit him at TimMyersStorySong.com.

**BONNIE PANG** is an award-winning illustrator and comic artist from Hong Kong. She holds a degree in Geography from the Chinese University of Hong Kong and a Master's in Fine Arts from the Academy of Arts University. Bonnie loves drawing animals and spreading positive vibes through her art. When she is not drawing, she can be found playing with her dog, cooking new dishes, and taking walks in nature. Visit her at bonniepangart.com.